Puffin Books
Editor: Kaye Webb

Magic at Midnight

Wild Duck on the inn sign couldn't believe his ears!
To think that he had spent over two hundred years,
night and day, stuck up there on the sign, when if
he'd only known what Hare from the *Hare and
Hounds* inn had just told him about the midnight
magic, he could have flown off every night from the
stroke of twelve till cock-crow!

'Hurry! Hurry!' called the hare over his shoulder,
and on the tenth stroke of the clock Wild Duck
moved gingerly, flapped his stiff wings up and
down, up and down, and dropped to the ground.
His first thought was to get to the pond, which he
could see from the inn sign during the winter when
the trees were bare, but he soon discovered other
delights in his nightly freedom, when he made
friends with Tawny Owl and other creatures like
Mermaid and Lion and Unicorn taking leave of
absence from their inn signs, and even interfering a
little in dangerous human affairs . . .

For readers of six and over.

Phyllis Arkle

Magic at Midnight

Illustrated by Eccles Williams

Puffin Books

Puffin Books: a Division of Penguin Books Ltd,
Harmondsworth, Middlesex, England
Penguin Books Inc., 7110 Ambassador Road,
Baltimore, Maryland 21207, U.S.A.
Penguin Books Australia Ltd, Ringwood,
Victoria, Australia
Penguin Books Canada Ltd,
41 Steelcase Road West, Markham, Ontario, Canada
Penguin Books (N.Z.) Ltd, 182–190 Wairau Road,
Auckland 10, New Zealand

First published by Brockhampton Press 1967
Published in Puffin Books 1974

Made and printed in Great Britain by
Cox & Wyman Ltd, London, Reading and Fakenham
Set in Monotype Baskerville

Contents

To Lynn

I Wild Duck has a surprise

Wild Duck on the inn sign couldn't believe his ears! He hadn't held a conversation with anyone for over two hundred years, but now the hare had stopped in his tracks and had spoken to him.

'For goodness' sake, get down,' the hare repeated. 'I've told you I'm tired of seeing you stuck up there every time I come past. Don't you know that when the clock is striking midnight – and only then – *anything* can move and be active until cock-crow?'

Wild Duck jerked his head in amazement – and found he could move. The hare grew impatient. 'Hurry up, slow-coach, or the chimes will have finished and you won't be *able* to get off. I'm the hare from *The Hare and Hounds* inn sign half a mile away, and I'm off and away as soon as I hear the first stroke of midnight. The hounds, stupid things, have never tumbled to the fact that they also could get down. And I'm not going to tell them. No fear!'

Many animals passed underneath *The Wild Duck* inn sign during the night, but now he came to think of it, Wild Duck realized that it was only at midnight and at cock-crow that he had seen this particular hare. Regular as clockwork he was, just as, for the past two years, Dan the farmer's boy had gone by at exactly half past five in the morning.

'Hurry! Hurry!' called the hare over his shoulder as he rushed off down the street. 'Don't miss your chance this time.'

On the tenth stroke of the clock, Wild Duck moved gingerly, flapped his stiff wings up and down, up and down, and dropped to the ground. It couldn't be true. Over two hundred years, night and day, he had spent up there on the inn sign, and had he but known about the midnight magic, he could have flown off every night! He looked up at the empty sign and – being a very conscientious bird – he reminded himself that he must be back on duty well before cockcrow.

He staggered down the road on legs unsteady through lack of exercise and then, to avoid the grit which cut into his webbed feet, he waddled on to the grass verge and made his way slowly, oh, so very slowly, towards the village. His first thought was to get to the pond, which he could see from the inn sign during the winter when the trees were bare. Head nodding and yellow beak opening now and then in a feeble quack, he stepped like a little old man through the trees and down the bank to the water's edge.

Wild Duck put one foot in the water and quickly withdrew it. Ouch! It was cold! Then be tried again, put in the other foot and waded into deeper water. As he got used to the cold he paddled off towards the middle of the pond. Just like sitting on an air cushion, he thought, delighted. It was wonderful. He'd never enjoyed anything so much in all his long life. He must do this every night. Exercise was so good for one.

He'd taken one awkward turn round the pond, feeling his limbs becoming more supple at every paddle, when he heard a rustling noise from the branch of a tree overhanging the water.

'Hoo-oo-oo-oo-oo-oo-ooh!' cried Tawny Owl, his eyelids blinking more rapidly than usual. 'Aren't you the wild duck from *The Wild Duck* inn sign? I thought I recognized your fine plumage. But, I must say, you look much handsomer on the water than you do on the sign. How did you manage to get here?'

'It's magic,' replied Wild Duck, his quack breaking in excitement. 'The hare told me only tonight that anything can move while the clock is striking midnight. But I've got to be back before cock-crow or, shiver my tail feathers, I

don't know what will happen to me.'
He swam off again joyfully.

'You're not a very good swimmer,'
commented Tawny Owl.

'You wouldn't be a very good flyer if
you'd been stuck on an inn sign for
years and years and years, would you,
now?' Wild Duck stood up in the water.
Then he immersed his head and
shoulders and, with tail pointing sky-
wards, he paddled furiously to keep his
balance. He soon surfaced, however.

'Good show!' approved Tawny Owl.
'You are having a good time, aren't
you? Sorry I can't join you, but I'm no
swimmer.'

'That's quite all right,' replied Wild
Duck politely. He had thought he had

15

the pond to himself, until he noticed a brown rat scrambling up the bank out of his way. Then a toad leaped out of the water and hurried off. A frog, with just his eyes showing out of the pond, peered at him suspiciously, and a fish popped its head up for a split second before dashing down again. They didn't trust him! Wild Duck turned sadly towards the bank.

But, 'It's all right, everyone,' called out Tawny Owl loudly. 'It's only Wild Duck from the inn sign and he won't eat you. It's his first outing for two hundred years!'

'Well, in that case I'd better say, "How-de-do and welcome to Silver Pond",' said Toad, turning back.

'Yes, of course,' said Frog and Brown Rat together. Fish appeared again. 'We'll be glad to see you on the bottom any time,' he said hospitably.

'You're all very kind, I'm sure,' said Wild Duck.

Just then the moon came out from behind a cloud and Wild Duck could see how the pond got its name. It looked like a silver saucer set among the trees. He began splashing about, dabbling in the water with his beak, trying to catch the moon's reflection and everyone laughed at him and joined in the frolicking. Led by Toad they played 'tick', chasing Wild Duck round and round the pond, until he felt quite exhausted and was glad to scramble up the bank and rest

under Tawny Owl's tree. They all gathered round in a circle and Tawny Owl
opened wide his big black eyes.

'You must build a nest in the reeds
and stay with us always. Then we can
have lots of fun,' he said.

'That's a very tempting offer,' replied
Wild Duck, who was resting with his
head tucked well down between his
shoulders, 'but I must be on duty during
the day-time. It wouldn't do to leave the
inn sign without its wild duck.'

'What does it feel like being stuck up
there all the time?' asked Frog. 'I'd be
bored stiff.'

Wild Duck's eyes flashed and he
ruffled his feathers. 'Not at all. I've got
a job to do the same as anyone else and,

if I may say so, I think I carry it out to everyone's satisfaction. *The Wild Duck* inn is well known all over the country. It began as a hostel hundreds of years ago, before my time, and many famous people have lodged under its roof. And the sign has been much admired.'

They were all impressed.

Wild Duck lowered his voice a little. 'Another thing – I've never before told this to any other living creature, but there's something of considerable value in *The Wild Duck* inn.' He paused dramatically. 'A long, long time ago, a soldier, carrying a parcel, came to the inn and I heard him ask the innkeeper to look after it for him while he was away at the wars. But the soldier never returned, perhaps he was killed in battle, I don't know, and the innkeeper died without telling anybody about it.'

'But what is "it"?' asked Toad impatiently.

'It's a picture.'

'A picture!' exclaimed Brown Rat in disgust.

Tawny Owl stirred himself. 'A picture

can be a very valuable object to human beings,' he said reprovingly. 'Surely you know that. Think of it, probably hundreds of years old and painted by a famous artist of the time. It would fetch thousands of pounds at an auction today – might even end up in the National Gallery.'

'Well, what's so mysterious about it?' asked Toad. 'Can't everyone see it if it's hanging on a wall?'

'Ah, ha,' replied Wild Duck. 'It's hanging on a wall in the dining-room, but the exciting thing is that the masterpiece is *underneath* a very ordinary painting of two cows in a field, and it would take an expert to strip off the outside paint and show what's beneath it.'

'Well, fancy that in our village,' marvelled Brown Rat.

'You mustn't tell anyone else about it,' said Wild Duck, beginning to wonder if it would have been wiser to have kept the secret to himself. 'But you've all been so generous to me tonight, I felt I wanted to share my secret with you.'

Wild Duck noticed a faint pearly grey in the sky. The cock would start crowing soon. 'I'm afraid I must be going back to the inn,' he said. 'Thank you all for giving me such a wonderful time.'

'Don't mention it,' they replied. 'We'll see you just after midnight tomorrow, and in the meantime we'll think up some more games.'

'I do appreciate it,' said Wild Duck. 'I'm rather ancient and – er – well – different from you all.'

'Oh, you don't look old and you'll soon be able to get about as quickly as anyone,' said Frog. 'Mind you, don't be surprised to find your limbs stiff and painful after the exercise. It'll wear off after a night or two, you'll see.'

Wild Duck started off through the trees.

'Just a minute,' called Tawny Owl.

'Did you say *anything* could move at midnight if it knew about the magic?'

'Well, the hare told me so. Why?'

'Never mind,' replied Tawny Owl in his wisest and most solemn voice. 'But I think I can promise that we'll have a surprise for you tomorrow night. See you then. You'd better hurry, hadn't you?'

As Wild Duck waddled down the road, something brushed past at great speed. 'Had a good time?' asked the hare. 'Glad you're taking advantage of the magic,' and he was gone.

Wild Duck reached the inn as the cock began to crow. He gave a flip, flap, flip of his wings, and became airborne just long enough to reach his place on the sign. He wasn't quite in position when the cock ceased to crow – and he was stuck again.

At half past five in the morning Dan came along on his way to the farm. Now it was generally assumed that the boy was a bit simple, but in fact he knew a great deal more about most things than people imagined. Dan glanced up at the inn sign and stopped walking. He went closer to the post and took another look.

'Goodness gracious me!' he murmured. 'How very strange!' and he banged on the door of the inn. When he received no answer he tried again, louder this time.

A bedroom window opened and Mr Short, the innkeeper, stuck his head out of the window. 'Now then, Dan, what do you want at this unearthly hour?' he asked querulously.

26

'Mr Short, sir, please, I thought you ought to know that your wild duck on the sign is looking in the wrong direction.'

Mr Short's face went purple. 'What utter nonsense!' he shouted, shaking his fist at Dan. 'Be off with you. Go and attend to Farmer Thomas's cows. Wrong way indeed. What next!' The head disappeared from view and the window was slammed shut.

Dan shrugged his shoulders and pushed his cap farther back from his blue eyes. He was well used to people not believing what he told them. Mr Short didn't even bother to glance at the sign that day and no one else noticed that Wild Duck was looking east towards the old almshouses, instead of west towards the church.

As for Wild Duck, he thought guiltily that he really must get back in good time tomorrow and settle in his proper position.

2 Down at the pond

At the first stroke of midnight the next night Wild Duck flew down to the ground. Yes, he flew down. Still feeling very stiff, he was, nevertheless, more confident and had set off briskly down the road when the hare came abreast of him. 'Glad to see you're off again. You'll be flying down to the pond soon,' said the hare, disappearing into the distance.

Wild Duck was excited. He would have liked to have given a little hop, skip and a jump as he went along, but he didn't know how. He was wondering what surprise awaited him. A present perhaps, or a special game, or even a midnight supper party.

When he arrived at the pond's edge, he was disappointed because Tawny Owl was not on his special perch. There was no one else in sight as Wild Duck waded into the shallow water. He quack, quacked hopefully, and there was an immediate response. Fish surfaced for a minute and others followed. There were scurrying noises around the pond, and soon Brown Rat, Toad and Frog, followed by several other small creatures, appeared. Wild Duck was very glad to see them all.

'Where's Tawny Owl?' he inquired.

'Oh, he's gone off on a mysterious errand. He said he'd be back soon,' explained Brown Rat.

'I am back,' and there was Tawny Owl on his branch. No one had heard him flying in. 'Don't look round until I tell you, Wild Duck,' he ordered.

The others stared in amazement. Then Wild Duck felt a hot breath on his neck and heard a sort of purring, grunting, growling. If this was to be the present, or whatever it was, he didn't think he was going to like it! When he was allowed to turn round and look, he nearly jumped out of his feathers.

'Don't panic,' called out Tawny Owl. 'It's only Lion from the sign of *The Lion*

and Fiddle inn. You need only look into
his beautiful rusty-coloured eyes to know
that he's absolutely trustworthy.'

Lion put down the bow and fiddle,
which be had been carrying in his
mouth, and with tongue lolling out, he
sat back on his haunches and looked
round at everyone. Wild Duck thought
that as the surprise was meant for him,

he had better be the first to greet Lion.

'Well, I'm extremely delighted to meet a fellow inn sign creature,' he said courteously. 'I suppose Tawny Owl flew over and told you about the midnight magic?'

'Yes, and you could have knocked me down with a human hair. I haven't yet got over the wonder of it. But, oh, my goodness, I was stiff when I climbed down the post. Actually, I fell the last two feet, and when I started to walk here' – he rolled his eyes and groaned – 'my legs felt just like wooden stilts.'

Wild Duck warmed to him. He certainly appeared to be a very affable lion. 'You'll soon lose the stiffness after some exercise. You should have seen me

33

struggling back last night, but I feel much easier now.'

Tawny Owl was rocking backwards and forwards on his big feet. 'As I appear to be Master of Ceremonies, might I suggest we have a dance, if Lion will be so kind as to play a tune on his fiddle?'

Lion's head drooped and he looked ashamed. 'The fact is, I can't play the fiddle,' he confessed. 'I don't know a "G" string from an "A" string. It's true that I've been holding the bow and fiddle for over a hundred years, but I think someone must have painted them on the inn sign as a joke. Certainly I've got no ear for music.'

'How very odd,' exclaimed Brown Rat. 'But there's a *Cat and Fiddle* inn in the next village, perhaps the cat could play a tune for us tomorrow night?'

'Or what about *The Ring o' Bells*? We could do a jolly jig to a peal of bells,' suggested Toad.

'And there's *The Pig and Whistle* on the other side of the common,' said Frog.

'Or *The Harp* – over the hill,' added Fish.

'Who's going to play the harp?' asked Brown Rat scornfully.

'Well, if you don't want me to stay, I'd better be getting back to my inn sign,' said Lion huffily, turning away.

'Oh, please, please, don't go. Not now, just when I've met you,' begged Wild Duck.

'Don't listen to them – they've forgotten their manners,' said Tawny Owl. 'Certainly you must stay. You're our guest of honour tonight. It really doesn't matter about the fiddle. We'll make our own music – we'll have a sing-song instead.'

But Lion wasn't listening. He'd gone into a crouch. His ears lay flat against his head and his tail went flick, flick, flick over his back. Wild Duck looked across at the undergrowth on the other side of the pond and saw the white tip of a tail moving. His heart missed a beat or two when he saw a fox emerging. Talk about a sitting duck! The fox was coming for him all right!

But Lion had sidled round the pond, and giving a great leap and a mighty

roar, he playfully rolled the fox over and
over into the bushes. As for the fox,
never before having seen anything so
fierce as a fully grown lion, as soon as he
was able, he scrambled up and dashed
away hotfoot to his lair. Lion came
sauntering back.

'You're very brave,' said Wild Duck
admiringly. 'I'll never be afraid of anything when you're around.'

'That fox couldn't catch a fly. He's been feeding on mushrooms and berries for ages,' said Tawny Owl. 'However, now that he's been dealt with, what shall we sing? Lion, you're the guest, you must choose.'

Lion gazed longingly at the silvery surface of the water. 'After all those years on the inn sign, I'd prefer to have a swim,' he said. 'It would be most refreshing.'

'I didn't know lions could swim,' said Fish.

'Don't show your ignorance,' reproved Tawny Owl. 'They swim across rivers in Africa, don't they?'

'Oh, but don't they get eaten up by crocodiles?'

'We lions choose carefully at which point to cross a river. We're not stupid enough to swim in deep water where an old croc or two might be lurking.' So saying, Lion plunged in. And what a splash there was as, muscles rippling and mane flowing in the wake of the water, he swam across the pond. Wild Duck followed and after a paddle round to limber up, he flapped his wings to show off the blue and white streaks, and then, neck stretched straight in front, he flew round and round Lion's head, skidding back on to the water like a water skier.

'My, my, how you've improved since last night,' commented Tawny Owl – and the others agreed.

After a time Lion struggled ashore.

'Phew! I'm not as lively as I thought I'd be,' he said, flopping down.

Wild Duck waddled fussily out of the water. 'Don't worry. I've told you, you'll be quite all right by tomorrow night. You'll see,' and he squatted down by Lion, and everyone gathered round for a chat. Tawny Owl said, 'Wild Duck has got a valuable picture, which no one knows about (except us, of course) at his inn. Is there anything interesting at *The Lion and Fiddle* inn?'

'Not that I know of,' sighed Lion. 'If there is anything valuable hidden in the inn, Mr Hurst, my innkeeper, would certainly like to know about it. He's not been doing too well lately. His father, when he died, left very little money, and there were a lot of debts. I'm very worried because Mr Hurst is such a kind-hearted man, and another thing, if the inn has to close, I'll lose my job.'

'Oh, what a shame,' cried Wild Duck. 'I wish we could move the picture to *The Lion and Fiddle* inn, but I suppose that's impossible.'

'I've just remembered. There's a well underneath the passageway of the inn,' added Lion. 'But that's not unusual. I understand there are lots of wells and underground passages in old inns.'

Time went all too quickly as they talked, and soon Wild Duck saw that the sky was getting lighter. They must be returning to their inn signs. It would take Lion, burdened with bow and fiddle, all his time to be back in position before cock-crow. So, reluctantly, Wild Duck and Lion said farewell to everyone.

'See you both tomorrow night,' said Tawny Owl. 'And don't forget to bring your fiddle, Lion. I think I can promise you we'll have some music.'

'Now, what's he got in mind?' asked Wild Duck. Lion just shook his head. It wasn't polite to speak with a mouth full of bow and fiddle.

'Well, good-bye everyone, and thank you for another entertaining night,' said Wild Duck, and Lion nodded his head vigorously. Wild Duck waddled off through the trees, and Lion swaggered along in the other direction. The hare came speeding past Wild Duck. 'I've just seen Lion from *The Lion and Fiddle* inn. What on earth have I started?' he called out.

Wild Duck was back in position on the sign in good time, but Lion had difficulty in climbing up the post, and he was not quite ready when the cock ceased its early morning call – and he was stuck again.

Dan came past *The Lion and Fiddle* inn

at his usual hour and glanced up at the inn sign. He stopped short. 'Mercy on me!' he exclaimed. 'Just look at that,' and he went up to the post and, jumping up with arm outstretched, felt something with his finger tips. Then he knocked on the door of the inn and kept on knocking until the innkeeper opened it.

'Mr Hurst, sir, I must tell you that your lion's tail is hanging at least two inches below the sign. I've felt it and it's all furry!'

Mr Hurst was really an easy-going man, but it was very early in the morning and he hadn't had his proper sleep.

'Haven't I got enough worries, what with bad debts and lack of customers

and everything, without you coming and waking me up with such a cock-and-bull story? Be off with you, there's a good lad.'

Dan sighed as he walked away. No one ever believed him. Mr Hurst forgot all about the matter, although during the day he remembered that he had had a frightful nightmare and had dreamed he had heard a lion roaring over by the pond. No one else bothered to look closely at the sign that day.

But Lion was worried. He'd have to start back a little earlier tomorrow. It was most undignified having the tuft at the end of his tail waving about in the breeze all day long!

3   Music at night

Next night, Wild Duck raced along the
road and was nearing the trees around
the pond before the hare caught up
with him. 'I'm wondering what you'll
get up to tonight,' said the hare in
passing. Wild Duck had a shrewd idea
what the surprise would be this time,
but he wasn't really sure.

There was no one in sight when he
arrived at the pond, so he gave his usual

quacking call and soon the pond folk came bustling around him. 'Where's Tawny Owl gone this time? And where's my friend Lion?' asked Wild Duck anxiously.

Fish popped up his head. 'Tawny Owl won't be long. He said he was going to bring along another guest.'

'I'm coming,' called Tawny Owl from a distance, 'and I'm bringing tonight's guest of honour.'

Wild Duck could faintly see Lion striding towards him – but who was that reclining gracefully on his back and holding tightly on to his golden mane? And just look at Tawny Owl perched comfortably on top of Lion's head! Wild Duck ruffled his wing feathers and quacked excitedly. He knew it! He knew it! He had guessed rightly. It was Mermaid from *The Mermaid* inn across the green. And how clever of Tawny Owl to have called first for Lion and hurried him off to *The Mermaid* inn before the chimes of midnight had ceased.

'I'm worn out,' announced Tawny Owl, flying on to his branch. 'What a rush I had getting from *The Lion and Fiddle* inn to *The Mermaid* inn in such a short time.'

With a grunt Lion dropped the bow and fiddle. 'What about me?' he retorted. 'As soon as I understood what you wanted me to do, I crossed the green – as the crow flies – in two or three leaps.' He looked up at Mermaid. 'But I'll do it every night for years and years, or for ever and ever, if necessary.'

'You needn't be in such a hurry an-other time,' answered Mermaid shyly. 'Now I know about the midnight magic, I'll slide down the post and wait for you.' Lion strolled across to the pond's edge and Mermaid dismounted and seated herself on a boulder – a substitute for a dolphin's back. Her long straight fair hair hung below her waist over the silvery scales and reached almost to her fin. Her sea-blue eyes sparkled and her coral red lips were curved in a smile.

'Well, go on, Wild Duck, say "Hello",' suggested Tawny Owl.

Wild Duck looked away, and then looked back at her. Never before had he seen anybody quite so beautiful. Mermaid gave him a special smile and he quacked feebly in greeting.

'He's shy!' teased Tawny Owl.

'I'm not! I'm not!' And with white-tipped tail feathers fluttering, Wild Duck paddled frantically across the pond. He wasn't away very long, however, as he couldn't bear to miss anything.

'Gather round, all of you,' invited Tawny Owl, and everyone came forward and made a ring round the sea-maid. It was evident that Tawny Owl was in his element directing the proceedings. 'Now we're all together,' he cried, 'may I say how pleased we are to welcome Mermaid to Silver Pond?'

'Hear, hear,' they all agreed.

'We are all hoping you will oblige us by playing a tune on the fiddle, Mermaid,' he continued, 'as unfortunately Lion is no musician.'

Wild Duck spoke up. 'Perhaps Mermaid would like to rest for a while. You remember how stiff and tired we were when we first got off our signs, Lion?'

'That's very thoughtful of you, Wild Duck,' replied Mermaid, 'but I'm quite all right, thank you. Don't think me rude, but I'm not nearly so old as you. I haven't been on the inn sign very long.'

'That's true,' agreed Tawny Owl. 'I've often wondered how you got on the sign in the first place, as we're a long way from the sea.'

'Well, my innkeeper was a sailor before he took over *The Mermaid* inn, and as he likes to be reminded of his sailing days, he altered the name from *The King's Arms* to *The Mermaid* – and that's when I came to be painted on to the sign.'

'Is he a good landlord?' asked Lion.

'Oh, yes, indeed, he's a very kind man,' she replied.

'So is mine,' said Lion. 'But he's getting very despondent, what with lack of money and not having very good health through worrying too much.'

'You're really bothered about him, aren't you?' said Wild Duck sympathetically. 'I do wish we could help him in some way.'

'We went into that last night and it isn't in our power, so let's get on with the sing-song, if Mermaid is ready,' said Tawny Owl.

Mermaid picked up the fiddle and began plucking at the strings. Everything became still, the wind ceased its bustling among the leaves, and the moon's reflection rested like a silver medal on the surface of the pond. Even the tips of the spiky pondweed flowers appeared to lean towards Mermaid.

'I think I could manage a lyre better,' she said, 'but if you'll hand me the bow, please, Lion, I'll see what I can do with a fiddle.' Lion picked up the bow in his mouth, and as Mermaid took it from him, he licked her hand with his rough sand-papery tongue and sat down beside her. She drew the bow delicately across the strings and they all listened spellbound.

Wild Duck thought that never before had he been so happy. He could listen to the music all night, and all the next night and the next and the next . . . To think that after all those lonely years on the inn sign he had discovered two companions like himself – to say nothing of Tawny Owl and all the other small creatures. He might even come to like the fox in time, provided, of course, that Lion was always around.

Mermaid stopped playing and put down the fiddle. 'My hair is getting in the way,' she said, tossing back her long fair hair. 'Have you got anything – a piece of string, or perhaps a long dried blade of grass – I could tie it back with?' They all looked about them and Wild Duck, who had gone to search under the trees, noticed something in the long grass. He hurried back with a length of pink satin ribbon dangling

from his beak. 'Will this do?' he asked.

'It's just the very thing,' replied Mermaid, delighted, tying back her hair with the ribbon and finishing off with a neat bow. Then, accompanying herself on the fiddle, she sang song after song about the sea, until Wild Duck imagined he could taste the salt spray on his beak and hear the waves breaking against the rocks.

Once there was a rustling in the undergrowth. Perhaps it was the fox, thought Wild Duck, but Lion was far too comfortable, stretched fully out with head resting on his paws, to bother. Anyhow, Wild Duck could hardly blame the fox for wanting to have a peep at Mermaid, so he didn't take any notice.

The night passed all too quickly and this time it was Tawny Owl who hurried them off. 'Now then, you members of the Midnight Inn Sign Club, hadn't you better be getting back on duty?'

The Midnight Inn Sign Club! How lovely, thought Wild Duck. Fancy being a member of such an exclusive club.

Tawny Owl continued, 'I'm inviting another guest for tomorrow night.'

'I know who it will be! I know who it will be!' chanted Wild Duck, flapping up and down excitedly.

'Oh, well, we'll see about that, Mr Know-All,' replied Tawny Owl, a trifle put out.

Then an awful thought struck Wild Duck. 'Oh, oh, you wouldn't dream of getting the hounds off *The Hare and Hounds* inn sign, would you? Please don't do that. The hare would never forgive me.'

'Don't you worry your beautiful green head about that. I don't want a pack of hounds trooping over our territory any more than you do. Now, then, you'll be

59

late if you don't hurry. Lion's already gone off with Mermaid.'

As Wild Duck ran down the road, the hare passed, going like a rocket. 'Great heavens!' he exclaimed. 'I've just seen Lion *and* Mermaid – whatever next?'

Wild Duck got back in good time after all. And at *The Mermaid* inn, Lion, with Mermaid still on his back, stretched to his full height so that the sea-maid could climb back on to her sign. Then he sped across the green.

Dan came past *The Mermaid* inn on his way to the farm next morning. He looked up at the sign, stopped and went closer. Then he put down his lunch bag and climbed up the post. He touched

Mermaid's hair and shook his own head in bewilderment.

He slid down the post and then knocked hard on the door of the inn.

The door was soon opened, for Mr Tarr was an early riser. 'Mr Tarr, please, sir, I really feel you must know that your mermaid's hair is tied back with pink ribbon, and what's more, it's real ribbon. I've touched it and it's all smooth and satiny.'

The old mariner hitched up his trousers and looked at Dan. 'Suffering sea cooks!' he exclaimed. 'Now, you listen to me, my boy. I've sailed the seven seas for forty years, and never in all my experiences have I come across a mermaid with her hair tied back with ribbon, or with anything else for that matter – and I would certainly never allow my mermaid to do anything so silly. So set your compass farmwards, my lad.' He smiled pityingly at Dan and closed the door.

'Shiver my timbers,' said Dan, picking up his bag and slinging it over his shoulders. 'They all think they know better than me.'

Mermaid felt very self-conscious sitting up on the sign with her hair tied behind her back, but no one else noticed anything amiss, which goes to show how unobservant people can be.

4   Wild Duck is alarmed

The next night, as Wild Duck was on his way to the pond, the hare came alongside and slackened his pace to fit in with Wild Duck's waddle. 'Now, look here, Wild Duck,' he said. 'I'm glad you're enjoying yourself, but no nonsense about the hounds on my sign – or else . . .'

'Oh, no, don't you worry,' panted Wild Duck. 'We'll never tell the hounds about the midnight magic. It would spoil everything.'

'All right, just see you don't do anything stupid, that's all. 'Bye,' and he was off.

When Wild Duck arrived at the pond, he found everybody assembled to meet him and very soon Tawny Owl flew in as well. 'There's another guest on his way. Look!' and after Lion, with Mermaid riding on his back, came a white, majestic figure.

This time Wild Duck went forward to meet the guest and did the honours without being prompted by Tawny Owl. 'We're very pleased to welcome another member to the Midnight Inn Sign Club,' he said.

Unicorn inclined his shapely head, pointing his long, sharp, twisted horn at Wild Duck. 'I'm exceedingly pleased to

have been invited,' he said. 'I must admit I feel a little stiffness in the old joints, but Lion tells me I'll feel fine by tomorrow night.'

'Indeed you will,' replied Wild Duck. 'There's nothing like a little exercise to put new life into one after – let me see, how many years have you been on the inn sign?'

'Only one hundred and fifty-seven.'

Wild Duck was relieved to learn that he was still the senior member of the Club – perhaps one day he might even be elected Chairman. He stretched out his neck and flapped his wings at the thought, as he watched Mermaid settle herself on the boulder.

'As pretty as a picture, isn't she?' said Unicorn.

'Picture – that reminds me,' said Tawny Owl. 'Is there any buried treasure in your inn? Or purses of gold or anything else hidden away?'

Unicorn laughed. 'Not that I know of,' he said. 'My inn is a very ordinary, common - or - garden type of hostel. Why?'

Wild Duck started to tell Unicorn

about the picture in his inn, when he saw a now-familiar white-tipped tail on the other side of the pond, and he drew back sharply.

'What's the matter?' asked Unicorn. 'Oh, ha, ha, that wily old fox is frightening you, is he? Leave him to me.' Unicorn's tail went flick, flick, flick over his back, just like Lion's tail had the other night. Indeed, Unicorn's tail was like Lion's, strong and wiry with a tuft at the end. Unicorn trotted stealthily round the pond and then, making a great show of strength and fierceness, he leaped on top of the fox and rolled him over and over into the bushes. He tickled the animal in the ribs with his magic horn until the poor fox collapsed giggling and begging for mercy. As soon as he could, the fox – never before having seen a mythical creature like Unicorn – rushed away headlong.

'What were you saying about a picture?' asked Unicorn, coming back to the group. Tawny Owl related all that was known about the valuable painting hidden in *The Wild Duck* inn, and Lion had to have his say and tell Unicorn how worried and unhappy he felt about his innkeeper.

'Poor man,' murmured the sea-maid. 'Never mind, perhaps one day things will take a better turn for him.'

'Picture . . . picture . . .' mused Unicorn, who was lying down alongside Lion. 'That rings a bell in my mind.

Now, let me think. When did I hear something about a picture recently? You must excuse me. I can't think properly. It's the excitement of being here with you all. Ah – I've got it! It was this morning. Two men – I didn't like the look of them – stood under my inn sign. They pretended to be examining the framed menu card outside the front door . . .'

Unicorn paused. 'Go on, please,' urged Wild Duck. 'What did they say?'

'If I remember rightly one of them said, "According to this old letter and map, *The Wild Duck* is at the far end of the village – before you come to *The Hare and Hounds* inn. From here, we must go past *The Mermaid* inn and then

The Lion and Fiddle inn to reach the one we want," and off they strolled as though they were out for a morning's walk.'

'But what did they say about the picture?' asked Wild Duck.

'Do be patient, old chap, I'm coming to that. On their return, they again stopped underneath my sign and I heard one of them say, "It's quite likely that the picture, with another painting on top, is still hanging on a wall in the inn, or it may even be hidden in the cellar. Anyhow, we can ransack the place tomorrow night. Let's make it about half an hour after midnight, shall we? There'll be no one at home then," and they laughed – if you can call such a nasty cackling sort of noise, laughing.'

Wild Duck was very agitated. 'But why are they so sure there'll be no one at home tomorrow night?'

'I know why,' put in Tawny Owl.

'Don't you remember that the Farmers' Ball is being held in the village hall tomorrow night, and everyone, visitors included, has been invited. The policeman's going to have his work cut out keeping his eye on the whole village. It's just the night for a well-planned robbery.'

'Can't we do something?' asked Mermaid wistfully. 'If I were big and strong and fully human, I'd try to stop them somehow.'

'It's not a question of strength. We'll have to match cunning with cunning,' said Tawny Owl.

'How?' queried Wild Duck.

But Tawny Owl had closed his eyes and, head dropped well down between his shoulders, appeared to have fallen asleep.

Toad puffed himself up and suggested, 'What if I arranged with all my friends to make a barrier across the doorway of *The Wild Duck* inn and frighten the robbers away? Do you think that would work?' Wild Duck could not help being amused at the thought of the small creatures tackling two men.

'If I wanted to, I could shrivel up the men with my magic horn – but I don't think it would be wise,' said Unicorn.

And Lion said, 'If I wasn't burdened with this beastly bow and fiddle, I'd soon chase them away!'

Tawny Owl woke up and hooted loudly, startling them all. 'I've got an idea,' he announced. 'Midnight Inn Sign Club members if you'll please listen very carefully . . .'

Wild Duck's head was buzzing with excitement as he hurried back to the inn, and he was hardly conscious of the hare saying, 'Unicorn as well, eh? Well, now that you've got the lot from this village – except the hounds, of course – I hope you're satisfied.'

'Oh, yes, rather,' replied Wild Duck absently, flying up to his position on the inn sign.

Lion helped Mermaid to climb back on to her sign and himself got in position in good time. But Unicorn, it being his first outing ever, was not quite ready when the cock ceased to crow.

Dan's lanky figure came along as usual and he stopped outside *The Unicorn* inn. 'What in the world does he think he's doing?' he cried, looking up at Unicorn. He rang the doorbell of the inn and finally managed to wake the innkeeper, who put his head out of the bedroom window.

'Mr Stubbs, sir, it's an amazing thing, but your Unicorn is sitting back on his haunches, instead of standing up straight on his hind legs with his front hooves pawing the air!'

'Now, Dan,' said Mr Stubbs, controlling his temper with difficulty. 'I'll let you off, but if you come here again with such a nonsensical story and . . . and . . .' His voice rose to a scream

'. . . and wake me up at this unearthly hour, I'll have the law on you!' He shook his fist at Dan's retreating figure. Dan hurried. He had no desire to get at cross purposes with the village constable.

'These innkeepers can't see further than the ends of their noses,' he said glumly. And no one else that day looked beyond the end of his nose either, so Unicorn's position went unnoticed.

As for Unicorn, he thoroughly enjoyed resting all day, but he realized that he must be more careful in future. It wouldn't do at all to be discovered in a sitting position.

5   Tawny Owl's plan

It was vital that he remembered Tawny Owl's instructions, thought Wild Duck, as he flew down from the sign the next night as midnight struck. 'Go straight to *The Lion and Fiddle* inn,' that was it. So, half waddling and half flying, Wild Duck went down the road. He soon saw Lion hastening towards him, and as they met, the hare passed at full speed.

'Now what are you two up to?' he asked suspiciously, without waiting for an answer. After Wild Duck and Lion had greeted one another, they continued on their separate ways, Wild Duck to *The Lion and Fiddle* inn, and Lion to *The Wild Duck* inn.

Wild Duck had nearly reached the inn when he noticed something that gave him a shock, so turning round he flew back. 'Lion, Lion,' he called breathlessly. 'You've forgotten your bow and fiddle! You'll have to go back for them. Whoever heard of a 'Duck and Fiddle' inn?'

'Oh, hang it, so I have,' said Lion under his breath, and he turned and ran. He was back in no time.

At *The Lion and Fiddle* inn, Wild Duck flew up and settled himself on the empty sign. He wasn't stuck on, of course, but he balanced very well. It was quite a large sign. But Lion was having great difficulty in squeezing himself, to say nothing of the bow and fiddle, on to the smaller Wild Duck inn sign. However, he managed in the end and resigned himself to a long wait.

Sounds of music could be heard coming from the direction of the village hall, otherwise all was quiet, unless one counted the night noises which discerning people can always hear. But eventually Wild Duck heard footsteps approaching and a beam from a torch flashed twice. That would be the robbers

T–E

checking the inn signs as they passed first *The Unicorn* inn and then *The Mermaid* inn, thought Wild Duck, shivering with excitement. Well, we'll match strategy with strategy.

As the men came up to *The Lion and Fiddle* inn, the torch flashed for an instant on the sign. '*This* is *The Wild Duck* inn,' said one of them uncertainly, stopping underneath the sign.

'No, no, come on, do, we've no time to play around. This is *The Lion and Fiddle* inn according to the map. The next one is *The Wild Duck* inn.'

'It isn't. This is *The Wild Duck* inn. Look!' And the light shone on the sign again.

They both peered up at the sign.

'You're right. That's certainly a duck. Things look different at night, I suppose, but we'd better nip along to the next inn to make doubly sure,' and off they sprinted.

They returned very quickly. 'Can't imagine how we came to make such a mistake. I could have sworn *The Wild Duck* inn was the last but one in the village.'

'Well, it isn't, and we'd better hurry if we're going to get the picture and make a getaway before people start leaving the village hall.'

Wild Duck watched as, with a skeleton key, the men opened the front door of the inn, which the innkeeper had left unbolted and unbarred. As the door was

left open, Wild Duck could hear the men moving about inside. They spent a long time in the dining-room, apparently examining all the pictures, and Wild Duck heard disgusted exclamations when they returned to the hall. 'It's obviously not in there. I've scraped a bit of paint off each picture and there's nothing underneath any of them,' said one man.

'Well, come on, then, let's keep moving, or the dance will be over before we've made a thorough search of the place.' They looked carefully at the pictures hanging in the hall, and on the stairway and on the landing. Then they decided to go down into the cellar.

After ten minutes or so, Wild Duck heard them coming back into the hall, evidently very bad-tempered and frustrated. 'That old letter and map must have been a hoax. There's no valuable picture at *The Wild Duck* inn, that's certain. We'd better cut our losses and be off.'

'Wait a jiffy! What's this iron ring

doing here?' Wild Duck heard a rattling sound and for an instant couldn't make out what the men were up to. Then there came a creaking noise and 'It's another cellar,' cried one man exultantly. 'I guarantee this is where we'll find the picture. Down the ladder we go. I'll lead the way.'

Wild Duck was puzzled. Two cellars? Then he laughed to himself. No, of course, there was only one cellar. The men were climbing down the well Lion had spoken about! Indeed, they were going down with a vengeance, for there was a sudden sharp crack, and the men screamed as the ladder came away from its moorings and clattered and crashed to the bottom of the well with a terrific splash. And what shouting and yelling! Enough to wake the whole village if all the villagers, with the exception of a few elderly people and young children, were not dancing in the village hall.

Wild Duck was tempted to get down off the inn sign, but as the shouts were getting more frantic, he thought some-one was bound to hear sooner or later. And eventually footsteps could be heard approaching the inn. The policeman on his rounds, perhaps? Wild Duck sincerely hoped a torch wouldn't be played on the sign.

But it wasn't the policeman. It was Dan, who, bored with the dance, had come out for a breath of fresh air, a look at the starry moonlit sky and a swift glance around for some of the small nocturnal creatures he knew would be abroad.

As Dan approached the inn, he stopped whistling and, head on one side, listened. 'Funny,' he said, 'thought I heard shouting. Must have been mistaken – everybody's at the dance.' But the yelling became louder near *The Lion and Fiddle* inn. Having no need of a torch, being well accustomed to the moonlight, Dan glanced up at the inn sign.

'What on earth are *you* doing up there?' he asked incredulously. 'Where's Lion?' Wild Duck pretended he hadn't heard, and Dan, scratching his head in puzzled fashion, went inside the inn. He

switched on the hall light and going
down the passageway soon discovered
the open trapdoor.

He knelt down and peered into the
well. Moans and groans and pleas for
help continued, and, by staring very
hard, Dan could see two white blobs
right at the bottom of the well.

'Whatever are you doing down there
at this time of night?' he asked inno-

cently. Being such an honest fellow him-self, he never suspected anyone of treachery.

'We were looking for something, but the ladder broke as we were climbing down. We didn't know there was water down here,' said one.

'And a brick fell out from the side of the well and oh, oh, what a bump I've got on my head,' groaned the other, splashing about in the water.

'Are you drowning?' asked Dan sym-pathetically.

'No, no, there's only a foot or so of water, but it's freezing cold and we're all bruised and cut. Go and get a ladder or a rope or something, for pity's sake.'

'Oh, I don't know where to look for a rope or a ladder long enough to reach to the bottom of this well. It's terribly deep, I know that.'

'Well, for goodness' sake, go and tell someone we're trapped down here,' said one man in despair.

'They wouldn't listen to me. They never believe anything I tell them,' said Dan simply.

He was just going to get up off his knees when he noticed a hole in the side of the well where the brick had been dislodged and, leaning over the side, he carefully pulled out a large square tin box. 'That's funny,' he said, sitting down on the floor with the box on his lap. 'I've found a tin box.'

'Oh, never mind about boxes,' they wailed. 'Go and get help. We'll have pneumonia at least after this.'

'I've told you – they'll never believe me,' answered Dan, busily opening the box. Taking out the contents, he placed them on the floor beside him. There were several bundles of bank-notes as well as other important-looking papers, and when he turned a small canvas bag upside down, dozens of golden sovereigns spilled out over the floor.

'My, my, Mr Hurst will be overjoyed when he hears about this,' Dan called down the well. 'It will make all the difference to his life. He'll be able to make the inn shipshape again, and attract lots of visitors.'

'Oh, why can't you go and get help? *Please* go.'

Dan had a sudden thought. He was really quite clever when he put his mind to it. Now, if he went to the village hall and told Mr Hurst that there were two men down his well, he wouldn't take any notice. Ah, ha, no, *but* this time Dan had evidence that what he was saying was true. When Mr Hurst saw the box and examined the contents, he would have to believe his own eyes.

And that is exactly what happened. Mr Hurst wouldn't listen to Dan at first. 'Another cock-and-bull story, eh, Dan?' he said, his eyes twinkling, but when Dan put the box into his hands and it was opened, Mr Hurst exclaimed, 'So

this is where my father hid all his money!'

The band stopped playing, everyone gathered round, and when Dan told them what had happened, they all ran along to *The Lion and Fiddle* inn.

In the meantime, as soon as Dan's back was turned, Wild Duck flew down and raced back to *The Wild Duck* inn. He quacked for Lion to get down quickly and, grumbling and complaining at his cramped position, Lion slid down the post. He soon cheered up, however, when he heard the news.

'Yes, yes, I'm telling you, there must be a small fortune in that box,' cried Wild Duck.

'Well, well. Best bit of news I've heard this century,' beamed Lion. 'And we must thank you for it.'

'Oh, no. It was Tawny Owl's idea that we changed places,' replied Wild Duck modestly.

'That's true, but if you hadn't been quick enough to get off your sign in the first place when the hare told you about

95

the midnight magic, none of us would have known anything about it, and your picture would have been stolen, and old Mr Hurst's hoard would never have been discovered.'

'Quick – back to your own sign. I hear them coming,' urged Wild Duck. Lion leaped away, not forgetting his bow and fiddle this time.

They were back in position when a group of people, headed by Dan, came along. As they went past *The Wild Duck* inn, Dan looked up at the sign.

'Ha, ha, back again, are you?' he said. 'I know what happened – you changed places with Lion, didn't you, now?'

'What did you say, Dan?' asked Mr Hurst.

'Nothing, sir,' replied Dan innocently.

The hare came past just before cock-crow. He glanced up at Wild Duck. 'You look as if butter wouldn't melt in your mouth,' he commented. 'But I know you better than that!'

The cock crowed as usual and Wild Duck and Lion were stuck again – and all was normal, until the next night.

6 Dan is much wiser

The following night, all four members of the Midnight Inn Sign Club were off their signs before the second stroke of midnight had boomed out, and as Wild Duck flew down the road, the hare passed and skidded to a stop. 'I give up. I really do! I can't think what you lot were up to last night – but I haven't got time to stop and listen to an explanation,' and he disappeared.

Wonder what *he* does after midnight, thought Wild Duck. But he soon forgot all about the hare, what with the excitement down at the pond. Mermaid and Unicorn, who had stayed at their posts all last night, wanted to be told exactly what had happened.

Mermaid was so touched when she heard about Mr Hurst's good fortune that small tears like silver raindrops glistened in the corners of her eyes. 'I told you, Lion, didn't I, that everything would come all right in the end for Mr Hurst? And I'm sure he'll use the money wisely. And, I must say, you look much better yourself since you heard the news – your coat is more silky and your eyes are brighter.'

Lion drew himself up. 'I feel on top of my form, thank you, Mermaid,' he said.

'I'm good for my job on the inn sign for at least another two hundred years or so.'

But when Mermaid heard about Lion forgetting his fiddle, she laughed and laughed. 'I thought only women forgot things,' she said. 'I haven't yet remembered to take off the hair ribbon. I enjoy wearing it so much, but I must remove it before dawn comes.'

'And, oh, what a tight squeeze it was on *The Wild Duck* inn sign,' said Lion. 'I had to hold my breath for nearly an hour.'

'Oh, just listen to him – that's a tall tale!' Unicorn was wishing he'd been 'in' on all the excitement. 'You've got to breathe to live.'

'Well,' replied Lion. 'I just let out my breath a little bit at a time like this . . .' and he drew in a very deep breath and exhaled slowly, slowly with a h-i-s-s-i-n-g sound.

'The robbers and all the villagers dancing in the hall would have heard that,' said Unicorn disbelievingly.

'Now then, you two, don't argue. Let's get on with the festivities. Who's for a swim before we have some music?' asked Tawny Owl.

And would you believe it, they all – except Tawny Owl – plunged into the pond and the water splashed up to the second branch of the old spruce tree. Wild Duck noticed that even a hedge-hog had joined them. The moon pushed aside a large dark cloud so that she could see what was going on. It was agreed by all that there was no doubt whatsoever that Mermaid was the best swimmer and the most graceful and the swiftest and the one who could stay under the longest.

Afterwards Mermaid rested on the boulder, took up the fiddle and played and sang. What absolute enchantment, thought Wild Duck. His head sank lower into his chest and he felt as though he was living in a beautiful dream world. But, suddenly, he came back to reality and quacked in alarm. Lion and Unicorn looked up in surprise, but Mermaid stroked his head. 'What's the matter, Little Duck?' she asked. He nodded in the direction of the bushes, where a white blob could be seen. Mermaid gazed in doubt, but Lion, without moving his head, whispered, 'It's not the fox. It's only Dan – take no notice. Go on playing, Mermaid, please.' So Mermaid played and sang a haunting lyric about mermaids and dolphins and fascinating creatures that live in the sea.

It was indeed Dan. He had crouched behind a bush and was watching enthralled at what was taking place in front of his eyes. He had suspected that there was some magic in the air and had promised himself that tonight he would get to the bottom of it.

He was still there when the first frail light of morning appeared, and not until he saw Wild Duck and Lion, fiddle and bow in his mouth and with Mermaid riding on his back, and Unicorn rush off towards their respective inns, did he make his own way homewards and get quietly back into bed for a short spell.

The members of the Midnight Inn

Sign Club had, as usual, been unwilling to leave their meeting-place and had only just managed to get back on to their signs before cock-crow.

Dan was a little late going to work next morning, but he found time to glance up at the sign of *The Unicorn* inn, the first one he came to. He grinned widely. 'Sitting down again, are you?'

he said. 'You must learn to be on duty in good time, old fellow, and be in your proper position,' and he passed on his way to work.

When he came to *The Mermaid* inn, late as he was, he couldn't resist climbing up the post and feeling the soft satin ribbon. 'Just like a woman,' he said. 'You'll have to remember to untie your hair before you report for duty, my beauty.' And he went on his way.

At *The Lion and Fiddle* inn, he jumped up delightedly and with the tips of his fingers gave the tuft of Lion's tail, which was hanging two inches below the sign, a gentle tweak. 'Most undignified,' he reproved. 'You must be more sprightly tomorrow.'

When he came to *The Wild Duck* inn, he shook his head. 'I know what's the matter with you,' he said. 'You're tired of looking to the west and want a change of scene. But you'll have to be gazing westwards again soon, before anybody notices what you're up to.'

Dan went serenely on his way, happy now that he knew all about magic at midnight. He hadn't knocked up any of the innkeepers this time. Oh, dear me, no, he knew better than to do a thing like that. They might now believe what he told them – and that would never do!

As he passed *The Hare and Hounds* inn, he deliberately refrained from raising his eyes to the sign post. He'd always known better than to interfere with anything a hare might be doing.

And all the villagers were so tired and bemused after the excitement of the previous night, that it never entered their heads to examine the inn signs, although there was speculation about the two men being trapped down the well of *The Lion and Fiddle* inn.

But the Midnight Inn Sign Club members spent an uneasy day on duty, and they all decided that they would be much more careful in future. They would be models of respectability and be on duty in their correct positions – and properly dressed! And so they were always – or nearly always!

About the Author

Phyllis Arkle was born and educated in Chester, but since 1959 has lived in the Thames valley village of Twyford in Berkshire. In addition to writing and reading, she is actively interested in the Women's Institute movement, and was recently President of the Twyford and Ruscombe W.I. Her other interests include music and bridge, and she is a patron of the Henley Symphony Orchestra. She is also engaged in voluntary work.

Mrs Arkle has had six books for children published by Brockhampton, and in connection with these she has studied the history of inn signs, dinosaurs, etc.

Some Young Puffin Originals

The Invisible Womble and Other Stories
Elisabeth Beresford

These five stories are retellings of some of the
television adventures and reveal the Wombles at
their funniest and best. This book will certainly
ensure their place in the family long after they
have left the studios and bolted the door of their
burrow behind them.

Olga Meets her Match
Michael Bond

More stories about Olga da Polga, the guinea-pig,
her friends Noel, Fangio and Graham, and a
fascinating new suitor, a Russian guinea-pig
prince named Boris.

Bad Boys
ed. Eileen Colwell

Twelve splendid stories about naughty boys, by
favourite authors like Helen Cresswell, Charlotte
Hough, Barbara Softly and Ursula Moray
Williams.

Duggie the Digger
Michael Prescott

As well as Duggie the Digger, there are tales about Horace the Helicopter, Bertram the Bus and Vernon the Vacuum Cleaner. It will please little boys who are interested in mechanical things.

Tales from the End Cottage
More Tales from the End Cottage
Eileen Bell

Two tabby cats and a peke live with Mrs Apple in a Northamptonshire cottage. They quarrel, have adventures and entertain dangerous strangers. A new author with a special talent for writing about animals.

The Young Puffin Book of Verse
Barbara Ireson

A deluge of poems about such fascinating subjects as birds and balloons, mice and moonshine, farmers and frogs, pigeons and pirates, especially chosen to please young people of 4 to 8.